I am an ARO PUBLISHING TEN WORD BOOK

My ten words are:

drops	of
water	clouds
are(is)	rain
snow	cold
ice	hard

Drops of Water

10 WORDS

Story and pictures by Bob Reese

BITTERSWEET SCHOOL IMC
P-H-M School Corporation
Mishawaka, Indiana

ISBN 0-89868-291-6—Library Bound
ISBN 0-89868-290-8—Soft Bound

Mmmm, drops of water.

Clouds.

Clouds are drops of water.

Rain.

Rain is drops

of water

Snow.

Snow is drops
of cold water

Ice.

Ice is hard drops of cold water.

Mmmm, drops
of water.